THE STELLAR LEGION

THE STELLAR LEGION

LEGION

by Leigh Brackett

No one had ever escaped from Venus' dread Stellar Legion. And, as Thekla the low-Martian learned, no one had ever betrayed it and—lived.

Silence was on the barracks like a lid clamped over tight-coiled springs. Men in rumpled uniforms—outlanders of the Stellar Legion, space-rats, the scrapings of the Solar System—sweated in the sullen heat of the Venusian swamplands before the rains. Sweated and listened.

The metal door clanged open to admit Lehn, the young Venusian Commandant, and every man jerked tautly to his feet. Ian MacIan, the white-haired, space-burned Earthman, alone and hungrily poised for action; Thekla, the swart Martian low-canaler, grinning like a weasel beside Bhak, the hulking strangler from Titan. Every quick nervous glance was riveted on Lehn.

The young officer stood silent in the open door, tugging at his fair mustache; to MacIan, watching, he was a trim, clean incongruity in this brutal wilderness of savagery and iron men. Behind him, the eternal mists writhed in a thin curtain over the swamp, stretching for miles beyond the soggy earthworks; through it came the sound every ear had listened to for days, a low, monotonous piping that seemed to ring from the ends of the earth. The Nahali, the six-foot, scarlet-eyed swamp-dwellers, whose touch was weapon enough, praying to their gods for rain. When it came, the hot, torrential downpour of southern Venus, the Nahali would burst in a scaly tide over the fort.

Only a moat of charged water and four electro-cannons stood between the Legion and the horde. If those things failed, it meant two hundred lives burned out, the circle of protective forts broken, the fertile uplands plundered and laid waste. MacIan looked at Lehn's clean, university-bred young face, and wondered cynically if he was strong enough to do his job.

Lehn spoke, so abruptly that the men started. "I'm calling for volunteers. A reconnaissance in Nahali territory; you know well enough what that means. Three men. Well?"

Ian MacIan stepped forward, followed instantly by the Martian Thekla. Bhak the Titan hesitated, his queerly bright, blank eyes darting from Thekla to Lehn, and back to MacIan. Then he stepped up, his hairy face twisted in a sly grin.

Lehn eyed them, his mouth hard with distaste under his fair mustache. Then he nodded, and said; "Report in an hour, light equipment." Turning to go, he added almost as an afterthought, "Report to my quarters, MacIan. Immediately."

MacIan's bony Celtic face tightened and his blue eyes narrowed with wary distrust. But he followed Lehn, his gaunt, powerful body as ramrod-straight as the Venusian's own, and no eye that watched him go held any friendship.

Thekla laughed silently, like a cat with his pointed white teeth. "Two of a kind," he whispered. "I hope they choke each other!" Bhak grunted, flexing his mighty six-fingered hands.

In his quarters, Lehn, his pink face flushed, strode up and down while MacIan waited dourly. It was plain enough what was coming; MacIan felt the old bitter defensive anger rising in him.

"Look," he told himself inwardly. "Books. Good cigars. A girl's picture on the table. You had all that once, you damn fool. Why couldn't you...."

Lehn stopped abruptly in front of him, grey eyes steady. "I'm new here, MacIan," he said. "But we've been Legion men for five generations, and I know the law; no man is to be questioned about his past. I'm going to break the law. Why are you here, MacIan?"

MacIan's white head was gaunt and stubborn as Tantallon Rock, and he kept silent.

"I'm trying to help," Lehn went on, "You've been an officer; every man in the barracks knows that. If you're here for any reason but failure in duty, you can be an officer again. I'll relieve you of special duty; you can start working for the examinations. No need to waste you in the ranks. Well?"

MacIan's eyes were hidden, but his voice was harsh. "What's behind this, Lehn? What the hell is it to you?"

The Venusian's level gaze wavered; for a moment the boy looked through the man, and MacIan felt a quick stab in his heart. Then all that was gone, and Lehn said curtly.

"If you find the barracks congenial stay there, by all means. Dismissed!"

MacIan glared at him half-blindly for a moment, his fine long hands clenching and unclenching at his sides. Then he 'bout faced with vicious smartness and went out.

*

Nearly an hour later he stood with the Martian Thekla on the earthworks, waiting. The monotonous pipes prayed on in the swamp; MacIan, looking up at the heavy sky, prayed just as hard that it would not rain. Not just yet. Because if it rained before the patrol left, the patrol would not leave; the Nahali would be on the march with the very first drop.

"And my chance would be gone," he whispered to himself.

Thekla's bright black eyes studied him, as they always did; an insolent, mocking scrutiny that angered the Scot.

"Well," he said dryly. "The perfect soldier, the gallant volunteer. For love of Venus, Thekla, or love of the Legion?"

"Perhaps," said Thekla softly, "for the same reason you did, Earthman. And perhaps not." His face, the swart, hard face of a low-canal outlaw, was turned abruptly toward the mist-wrapped swamp. "Love of Venus!" he snarled. "Who could love this lousy sweatbox? Not even Lehn, if he had the brains of a flea!"

"Mars is better, eh?" MacIan had a sudden inspiration. "Cool dry air, and little dark women, and the wine-shops on the Jekkara Low-canal. You'd like to be back there, wouldn't you?"

To himself, he thought in savage pleasure, "I'll pay you out, you little scum. You've tortured me with what I've lost, until I'd have killed you if it hadn't been against my plan. All right, see if you can take it!"

The slow dusk was falling; Thekla's dark face was a blur but MacIan knew he had got home. "The fountains in the palace gardens, Thekla; the sun bursting up over red deserts; the singing girls and the *thil* in Madame Kan's. Remember the *thil*, Thekla? Ice cold and greenish, bubbling in blue glasses?"

He knew why Thekla snarled and sprang at him, and it wasn't Thekla he threw down on the soft earth so much as a tall youngster with a fair mustache, who had goaded with good intent. Funny, thought MacIan, that well-intentioned goads hurt worse than the other kind.

A vast paw closed on his shoulder, hauling him back. Another, he saw, yanked Thekla upright. And Bhak the Titan's hairy travesty of a face peered down at them.

"Listen," he grunted, in his oddly articulated Esperanto. "I know what's up. I got ears, and village houses got thin walls. I heard the Nahali girl talking. I don't know which one of you has the treasure, but I want it. If I don't get it...."

His fingers slid higher on MacIan's shoulder, gripped his throat. Six fingers, like iron clamps. MacIan heard Thekla choking and cursing; he managed to gasp:

"You're in the wrong place, Bhak. We're men. I though you only strangled women."

The grip slackened a trifle. "Men too," said Bhak slowly. "That's why I had to run away from Titan. That's why I've had to run away from everywhere. Men or women—anyone who laughs at me."

MacIan looked at the blank-eyed, revolting face, and wondered that anyone could laugh at it. Pity it, shut it harmlessly away, but not laugh.

Bhak's fingers fell away abruptly. "They laugh at me," he repeated miserably, "and run away. I know I'm ugly. But I want friends and a wife, like anyone else. Especially a wife. But they laugh at me, the women do, when I ask them. And...." He was shaking suddenly with rage and his face was a beast's face, blind and brutal. "And I kill them. I kill the damned little vixens that laugh at me!"

He stared stupidly at his great hands. "Then I have to run away. Always running away, alone." The bright, empty eyes met MacIan's with deadly purpose. "That's why I want the money. If I have money, they'll like me. Women always like men who have money. If I kill one of you, I'll have to run away again. But if I have someone to go with me. I won't mind."

Thekla showed his pointed teeth. "Try strangling a Nahali girl, Bhak. Then we'll be rid of you."

Bhak grunted. "I'm not a fool. I know what the Nahali do to you. But I want that money the girl told about, and I'll get it. I'd get it now, only Lehn will come."

He stood over them, grinning. MacIan drew back, between pity and disgust. "The Legion is certainly the System's garbage dump," he muttered in Martian, loud enough for Thekla to hear, and smiled at the low-canaler's stifled taunt. Stifled, because Lehn was coming up, his heavy water-boots thudding on the soggy ground.

*

Without a word the three fell in behind the officer, whose face had taken on an unfamiliar stony grimness. MacIan wondered whether it was anger at him, or fear of what they might get in the swamp. Then he shrugged; the young cub would have to follow his own trail, wherever it led. And MacIan took a stern comfort from this thought. His own feet were irrevocably directed; there was no doubt, no turning back. He'd never have again to go through what Lehn was going through. All he had to do was wait.

The plank bridge groaned under them, almost touching the water in the moat. Most ingenious, that moat. The Nahali could swim it in their sleep, normally, but when the conductor rods along the bottom were turned on, they literally burned out their circuits from an overload. The swamp-rats packed a bigger potential than any Earthly electric eel.

Ian MacIan, looking at the lights of the squalid village that lay below the fort, reflected that the Nahali had at least one definitely human trait. The banging of a three-tiered Venusian piano echoed on the heavy air, along with shouts and laughter that indicated a free flow of "swamp juice." This link in the chain of stations surrounding the swamplands was fully garrisoned only during the rains, and the less warlike Nahali were busy harvesting what they could from the soldiers and the rabble that came after them.

Queer creatures, the swamp-rats, with their ruby eyes and iridescent scales. Nature, in adapting them to their wet, humid environment, had left them somewhere between warm-blooded mammals and cold-blooded reptiles, anthropoid in shape, man-sized, capricious. The most remarkable thing about them was their breathing apparatus, each epithelial cell forming a tiny electrolysis plant to extract oxygen from water. Since they lived equally on land and in water, and since the swamp air was almost a mist, it suited them admirably. That was why they had to wait for the rains to go raiding in the fertile uplands; and that was why hundreds of Interworld Legionnaires had to swelter on the strip of soggy ground between swamp and plateau to stop them.

MacIan was last in line. Just as his foot left the planks, four heads jerked up as one, facing to the darkening sky.

"Rain!"

Big drops, splattering slowly down, making a sibilant whisper across the swamp. The pipes broke off, leaving the ears a little deafened with the lack of them after so long. And MacIan, looking at Lehn, swore furiously in his heart.

The three men paused, expecting an order to turn back, but Lehn waved them on.

"But it's raining," protested Bhak. "Well get caught in the attack."

The officer's strangely hard face was turned toward them. "No," he said, with an odd finality, "they won't attack. Not yet."

They went on, toward the swamp that was worse in silence than it had been with the praying pipes. And MacIan, looking ahead at the oddly assorted men plowing grimly through the mud, caught a sudden glimpse of something dark and hidden, something beyond the simple threat of death that hung always over a reconnoitering patrol.

*

The swamp folded them in. It is never truly dark on Venus, owing to the thick, diffusing atmosphere. There was enough light to show branching, muddy trails, great still pools choked with weeds, the spreading *liha*-trees with their huge pollen pods, everything dripping with the slow rain. MacIan could hear the thudding of that rain for miles around on the silent air; the sullen forerunner of the deluge.

Fort and village were lost in sodden twilight. Lehn's boots squelched onward through the mud of a trail that rose gradually to a ridge of higher ground. When he reached the top, Lehn turned abruptly, his electro-gun seeming to materialize in his hand, and MacIan was startled by the bleak look of his pink, young face.

"Stop right there," said Lehn quietly. "Keep your hands up. And don't speak until I'm finished."

He waited a second, with the rain drumming on his waterproof coverall, dripping from the ends of his fair mustache. The others were obedient, Bhak a great grinning hulk between the two slighter men. Lehn went on calmly.

"Someone has sold us out to the Nahali. That's how I know they won't attack until they get the help they're waiting for. I had to find out, if possible, what preparations they have made for destroying our electrical supply, which is our only vulnerable point. But I had a double purpose in calling this party. Can you guess what it is?"

MacIan could. Lehn continued:

"The traitor had his price; escape from the Legion, from Venus, through the swamp to Lhiva, where he can ship out on a tramp. His one problem was to get away from the fort without being seen, since all leaves have been temporarily cancelled."

Lehn's mist-grey eyes were icy. "I gave him that chance."

Bhak laughed, an empty, jarring road. "See? That's what the Nahali girl said. She said, 'He can get what he needs, now. He'll get away before the rains, probably with a patrol; then our people can attack.' I know what he needed. Money! And I want it."

"Shut up!" Lehn's electro-gun gestured peremptorily. "I want the truth of this. Which one of you is the traitor?"

Thekla's pointed white teeth gleamed. "MacIan loves the Legion, sir. *He* couldn't be guilty."

Lehn's gaze crossed MacIan's briefly, and again the Scot had a fleeting glimpse of something softer beneath the new hardness. It was something that took him back across time to a day when he had been a green subaltern in the Terran Guards, and a hard-bitten, battle-tempered senior officer had filled the horizon for him.

It was the something that had made Lehn offer him a chance, when his trap was set and sprung. It was the something that was going to make Lehn harder on him now than on either Bhak or Thekla. It was hero-worship.

MacIan groaned inwardly. "Look here," he said. "We're in Nahali country. There may be trouble at any moment. Do you think this is the time for detective work? You may have caught the wrong men anyway. Better do your job of reconnoitering, and worry about the identity of the traitor back in the fort."

"You're not an officer now, MacIan!" snapped Lehn. "Speak up, and I want the truth. You, Thekla!"

Thekla's black eyes were bitter. "I'd as well be here as anywhere, since I can't be on Mars. How could I go back, with a hanging charge against me?"

"MacIan?" Lehn's grey gaze was levelled stiffly past his head. And MacIan was quivering suddenly with rage; rage against the life that had brought him where he was, against Lehn, who was the symbol of all he had thrown away.

"Think what you like," he whispered, "and be damned!"

*

Bhak's movement came so swiftly that it caught everyone unprepared. Handling the Martian like a child's beanbag, he picked him up and hurled him against Lehn. The electro-gun spat a harmless bolt into empty air as the two fell struggling in the mud. MacIan sprang forward, but Bhak's great fingers closed on his neck. With his free hand, the Titan dragged Thekla upright; he held them both helpless while he kicked the sprawling Lehn in the temple.

In the split second before unconsciousness took him, Lehn's eyes met MacIan's and they were terrible eyes. MacIan groaned, "You young fool!" Then Lehn was down, and Bhak's fingers were throttling him.

"Which one?" snarled the Titan. "Give me the money, and I'll let you go. I'm going to have the money, if I have to kill you. Then the girls won't laugh at me. Tell me. Which one?"

MacIan's blue eyes widened suddenly. With all his strength he fought to croak out one word: "Nahali!"

Bhak dropped them with a grunt. Swinging his great hands, forgetting his gun completely, he stood at bay. There was a rush of bodies in the rain-blurred dusk, a flash of scarlet eyes and triangular mouths laughing in queer, noseless faces. Then there were scaly, man-like things hurled like battering-rams against the Legionnaires.

MacIan's gun spat blue flame; two Nahali fell, electrocuted, but there were too many of them. His helmet was torn off, so that his drenched white hair blinded him; rubber-shod fists and feet lashed against reptilian flesh. Somewhere just out of sight, Thekla was cursing breathlessly in low-canal argot. And Lehn, still dazed, was crawling gamely to his feet; his helmet had protected him from the full force of Bhak's kick.

The hulking Titan loomed in the midst of a swarm of red-eyed swamp-rats. And MacIan saw abruptly that he had taken off his clumsy gloves when he had made ready to strangle his mates. The great six-fingered hands stretched hungrily toward a Nahali throat.

"Bhak!" yelled MacIan. "*Don't...!*"

The Titan's heavy laughter drowned him out; the vast paws closed in a joyous grip. On the instant, Bhak's great body bent and jerked convulsively; he slumped down, the heart burned out of him by the electricity circuited through his hands.

Lehn's gun spoke. There was a reek of ozone, and a Nahali screamed like a stricken reptile. The Venusian cried out in sudden pain, and was silent; MacIan, struggling upright, saw him buried under a pile of scaly bodies. Then a clammy paw touched his own face. He moaned as a numbing shock struck through him, and lapsed into semi-consciousness.

*

He had vague memories of being alternately carried and towed through warm lakes and across solid ground. He knew dimly that he was dumped roughly under a *liha*-tree in a clearing where there were thatched huts, and that he was alone.

After what seemed a very long time he sat up, and his surroundings were clear. Even more clear was Thekla's thin dark face peering amusedly down at him.

The Martian bared his pointed white teeth, and said, "Hello, traitor."

MacIan would have risen and struck him, only that he was weak and dizzy. And then he saw that Thekla had a gun.

His own holster was empty. MacIan got slowly to his feet, raking the white hair out of his eyes, and he said, "You dirty little rat!"

Thekla laughed, as a fox might laugh at a baffled hound. "Go ahead and curse me, MacIan. You high-and-mighty renegade! You were

14

right; I'd rather swing on Mars than live another month in this damned sweatbox! And I can laugh at you, Ian MacIan! I'm going back to the deserts and the wine-shops on the Jekkara Low-canal. The Nahali girl didn't mean money; she meant plastic surgery, to give me another face. I'm free. And you're going to die, right here in the filthy mud!"

A slow, grim smile touched MacIan's face, but he said nothing.

"Oh, I understand," said Thekla mockingly. "You fallen swells and your honor! But you won't die honorably, any more than you've lived that way."

MacIan's eyes were contemptuous and untroubled.

The pointed teeth gleamed. "You don't understand, MacIan. Lehn isn't going to die. He's going back to face the music, after his post is wiped out. I don't know what they'll do to him, but it won't be nice. And remember, MacIan, he thinks you sold him out. He thinks *you* cost him his post, his men, his career: his honor, you scut! Think that over when the swamp-rats go to work on you—they like a little fun now and then—and remember I'm laughing!"

*

MacIan was silent for a long time, hands clenched at his sides, his craggy face carved in dark stone under his dripping white hair. Then he whispered, "Why?"

Thekla's eyes met his in sudden intense hate. "Because I want to see your damned proud, supercilious noses rubbed in the dirt!"

MacIan nodded. His face was strange, as though a curtain had been drawn over it. "Where's Lehn?"

Thekla pointed to the nearest hut. "But it won't do you any good. The rats gave him an overdose, accidentally, of course, and he's out for a long time."

MacIan went unsteadily toward the hut through rain. Over his shoulder he heard Thekla's voice: "Don't try anything funny, MacIan. I can shoot you down before you're anywhere near an escape, even if you could find your way back without me. The Nahali are gathering now, all over the swamp; within half an hour they'll march on the fort, and then on to the plateaus. They'll send my escort before they go, but you and Lehn will have to wait until they come back. You can think of me while you're waiting to die, MacIan; me, going to Lhiva and freedom!"

MacIan didn't answer. The rhythm of the rain changed from a slow drumming to a rapid, vicious hiss; he could see it, almost smoking in the broad leaves of the *liha*-trees. The drops cut his body like whips, and he realized for the first time that he was stripped to trousers and shirt. Without his protective rubber coverall, Thekla could electrocute him far quicker even than a Nahali, with his service pistol.

The hut, which had been very close, was suddenly far off, so far he could hardly see it. The muddy ground swooped and swayed underfoot. MacIan jerked himself savagely erect. Fever. Any fool who prowled the swamp without proper covering was a sure victim. He looked back at Thekla, safe in helmet and coverall, grinning like a weasel under the shelter of a pod-hung tree-branch.

The hut came back into proper perspective. Aching, trembling suddenly with icy cold, he stooped and entered. Lehn lay there, dry but stripped like MacIan, his young face slack in unconsciousness. MacIan raised a hand, let it fall limply back. Lehn was still paralyzed from the shock. It might be hours, even days before he came out of it. Perhaps never, if he wasn't cared for properly.

MacIan must have gone a little mad then, from the fever and the shock to his own brain, and Thekla. He took Lehn's shirt in both hands and shook him, as though to beat sense back into his brain, and shouted at him in hoarse savagery.

"All I wanted was to die! That's what I came to the Legion for, to die like a soldier because I couldn't live like an officer. But it had to be honorably, Lehn! Otherwise...."

He broke off in a fit of shivering, and his blue eyes glared under his white, tumbled hair. "You robbed me of that, damn you! You and

Thekla. You trapped me. You wouldn't even let me die decently. I was an officer, Lehn, like you. Do you hear me, young fool? I had to choose between two courses, and I chose the wrong one. I lost my whole command. Twenty-five hundred men, dead.

"They might have let me off at the court-martial. It was an honest mistake. But I didn't wait. I resigned. All I wanted was to die like a good soldier. That's why I volunteered. And you tricked me, Lehn! You and Thekla."

He let the limp body fall and crouched there, holding his throbbing head in his hands. He knew he was crying, and couldn't stop. His skin burned, and he was cold to the marrow of his bones.

Suddenly he looked at Lehn out of bright, fever-mad eyes. "Very well," he whispered. "I won't die. You can't kill me, you and Thekla, and you go on believing I betrayed you. I'll take you back, you two, and fight it out. I'll keep the Nahali from taking the fort, so you can't say I sold it out. I'll make you believe me!"

From somewhere, far off, he heard Thekla laugh.

*

MacIan huddled there for some time, his brain whirling. Through the rain-beat and the fever-mist in his head and the alternate burning and freezing that racked his body, certain truths shot at him like stones from a sling.

Thekla had a gun that shot a stream of electricity. A gun designed for Nahali, whose nervous systems were built to carry a certain load and no more, like any set of wires. The low frequency discharge was strong enough to kill a normal man only under ideal conditions; and these conditions were uniquely ideal. Wet clothes, wet skin, wet ground, even the air saturated.

Then there were metal and rubber. Metal in his belt, in Lehn's belt; metal mesh, because the damp air rotted everything else. Rubber on his feet, on Lehn's feet. Rubber was insulation. Metal was a conductor.

MacIan realized with part of his mind that he must be mad to do what he planned to do. But he went to work just the same.

Ten minutes later he left the hut and crossed the soaking clearing in the downpour. Thekla had left the *liha*-tree for a hut directly opposite Lehn's; he rose warily in the doorway, gun ready. His sly black eyes took in MacIan's wild blue gaze, the fever spots burning on his lean cheekbones, and he smiled.

"Get on back to the hut," he said. "Be a pity if you die before the Nahali have a chance to try electro-therapy."

MacIan didn't pause. His right arm was hidden behind his back. Thekla's jaw tightened. "Get back or I'll kill you!"

MacIan's boots sucked in the mud. The beating rain streamed from his white hair, over his craggy face and gaunt shoulders. And he didn't hesitate.

Thekla's pointed teeth gleamed in a sudden snarl. His thumb snapped the trigger; a bolt of blue flame hissed toward the striding Scot.

MacIan's right hand shot out in the instant the gun spoke. One of Lehn's rubber boots cased his arm almost to the shoulder, and around the ankle of it a length of metal was made fast; two mesh belts linked together. The spitting blue fire was gathered to the metal circle, shot down the coupled lengths, and died in the ground.

The pistol sputtered out as a coil fused. Thekla cursed and flung it at MacIan's head. The Scot dodged it, and broke into a run, dropping Lehn's boot that his hands might be free to grapple.

Thekla fought like a low-canal rat, but MacIan was bigger and beyond himself with the first madness of fever. He beat the little Martian down and bound him with his own belt, and then went looking for his clothes and gun.

He found them, with Lehn's, in the hut next door. His belt pouch yielded quinine; he gulped a large dose and felt better. After he had dressed, he went and wrestled Lehn into his coverall and helmet and dragged him out beside Thekla, who was groaning back to consciousness in the mud.

Looking up, MacIan saw three Nahali men watching him warily out of scarlet eyes as they slunk toward him.

Thekla's escort. And it was a near thing. Twice clammy paws seared his face before he sent them writhing down into the mud, jerking as the overload beat through their nervous systems. Triangular mouths gaped in noseless faces, hand-like paws tore convulsively at scaly breast-plates, and MacIan, as he watched them die, said calmly:

"There will be hundreds of them storming the fort. My gun won't be enough. But somehow I've got to stop them."

No answer now. He shrugged and kicked Thekla erect. "Back to the fort, scut," he ordered, and laughed. The linked belts were fastened now around Thekla's neck, the other end hooked to the muzzle of MacIan's gun, so that the slightest rough pull would discharge it. "What if I stumble?" Thekla snarled, and MacIan answered, "You'd better not!"

Lehn was big and heavy, but somehow MacIan got him across his shoulders. And they started off.

*

The fringe of the swamp was in sight when MacIan's brain became momentarily lucid. Another dose of quinine drove the mists back, so that the fort, some fifty yards away, assumed its proper focus. MacIan dropped Lehn on his back in the mud and stood looking, his hand ready on his gun.

The village swarmed with swamp-rats in the slow, watery dawn. They were ranged in a solid mass along the edges of the moat, and the fort's guns were silent MacIan wondered why, until he saw that the dam that furnished power for the turbine had been broken down.

Thekla laughed silently. "My idea, MacIan. The Nahali would never have thought of it themselves. They can't drown, you know. I showed them how to sneak into the reservoir, right under the fort's guns, and stay under water, loosening the stones around the spillway. The pressure did the rest. Now there's no power for the big guns, nor the conductor rods in the moat."

He turned feral black eyes on MacIan. "You've made a fool of yourself. You can't stop those swamp-rats from tearing the fort apart. You can't stop me from getting away, after they're through. You can't stop Lehn from thinking what he does. You haven't changed anything by these damned heroics!"

"Heroics!" said MacIan hoarsely, and laughed. "Maybe." With sudden viciousness he threw the end of the linked belts over a low *liha*-branch, so that Thekla had to stand on tiptoe to keep from strangling. Then, staring blindly at the beleagured fort, he tried to beat sense out of his throbbing head.

"There was something," he whispered. "Something I was saying back in the swamp. Something my mind was trying to tell me, only I was delirious. What was it, Thekla?"

The Martian was silent, the bloody grin set on his dark face. MacIan took him by the shoulders and shook him. "What was it?"

Thekla choked and struggled as the metal halter tightened. "Nothing, you fool! Nothing but Nahali and *liha*-trees."

"*Liha*-trees!" MacIan's fever-bright eyes went to the great green pollen-pods hung among the broad leaves. He shivered, partly with chill, partly with exultation. And he began like a madman to strip Lehn and Thekla of their rubber coveralls.

Lehn's, because it was larger, he tented over two low branches. Thekla's he spread on the ground beneath. Then he tore down pod after pod from the *liha*-tree, breaking open the shells under the shelter of the improvised tent, pouring out the green powder on the groundcloth.

When he had a two-foot pile, he stood back and fired a bolt of electricity into the heart of it.

Thick, oily black smoke poured up, slowly at first, then faster and faster as the fire took hold. A sluggish breeze was blowing out of the swamp, drawn by the cooler uplands beyond the fort; it took the smoke and sent it rolling toward the packed and struggling mass on the earthworks.

Out on the battlefield, Nahali stiffened suddenly, fell tearing convulsively at their bodies. The beating rain washed the soot down onto them harder and harder, streaked it away, left a dull film over the reptilian skins, the scaly breast-plates. More and more of them fell as the smoke rolled thicker, fed by the blackened madman under the *liha*-tree, until only Legionnaires were left standing in its path, staring dumbly at the stricken swamp-rats.

The squirming bodies stilled in death. Hundreds more, out on the edges of the smoke, seeing their comrades die, fled back into the swamp. The earthworks were cleared. Ian MacIan gave one wild shout that carried clear to the fort. Then he collapsed, crouched shivering beside the unconscious Lehn, babbling incoherently.

Thekla, strained on tiptoe under the tree-branch, had stopped smiling.

The fever-mists rolled away at last. MacIan woke to see Lehn's pink young face, rather less pink than usual, bending over him.

Lehn's hand came out awkwardly. "I'm sorry, MacIan. Thekla told me; I made him. I should have known." His grey eyes were ashamed. MacIan smiled and gripped his hand with what strength the fever had left him.

"My own fault, boy. Forget it."

Lehn sat down on the bed. "What did you do to the swamp-rats?" he demanded eagerly. "They all have a coating as though they'd been dipped in paraffin!"

MacIan chuckled. "In a way, they were. You know how they breathe; each skin cell forming a miniature electrolysis plant to extract oxygen from water. Well, it extracts hydrogen too, naturally, and the hydrogen is continually being given off, just as we give off carbon dioxide.

"Black smoke means soot, soot means carbon. Carbon plus hydrogen forms various waxy hydrocarbons. Wax is impervious to both water and air. So when the oily soot from the smoke united with the hydrogen exuded from the Nahali's bodies, it sealed away the life-giving water from the skin-cells. They literally smothered to death, like an Earthly ant doused with powder."

Lehn nodded. He was quiet for a long time, his eyes on the sick-bay's well-scrubbed floor. At length, he said:

"My offer still goes, MacIan. Officer's examinations. One mistake, an honest one, shouldn't rob you of your life. You don't even know that it would have made any difference if your decision had been the other way. Perhaps there was no way out."

MacIan's white head nodded on the pillow.

"Perhaps I will, Lehn. Something Thekla said set me thinking. He said he'd rather die on Mars than live another month in exile. I'm an exile too, Lehn, in a different way. Yes, I think I'll try it. And if I fail again—" he shrugged and smiled—"there are always Nahali."

It seemed for a minute after that as though he had gone to sleep. Then he murmured, so low that Lehn had to bend down to hear him:

"Thekla will hang after the court-martial. Can you see that they take him back to Mars, first?"

www.ingramcontent.com/pod-product-compliance
Lightning Source LLC
Chambersburg PA
CBHW021006150626
46549CB00012BA/1383